STONE ARCH BOOKS
a capstone imprint

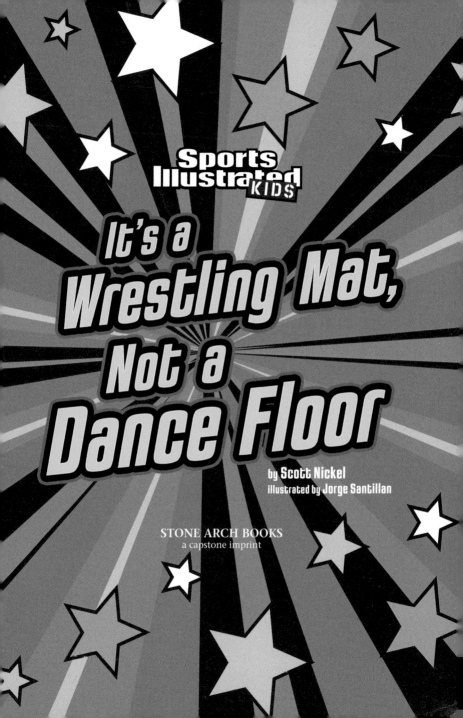

Sports Illustrated KIDS

It's a Wrestling Mat, Not a Dance Floor

by Scott Nickel

illustrated by Jorge Santillan

STONE ARCH BOOKS
a capstone imprint

VICTORY SCHOOL SUPERSTARS

Sports Illustrated KIDS *It's a Wrestling Mat, Not a Dance Floor* is published by Stone Arch Books —
A Capstone Imprint
151 Good Counsel Drive, P.O. Box 669
Mankato, Minnesota 56002
www.capstonepub.com

Art Director and Designer: Bob Lentz
Creative Director: Heather Kindseth
Production Specialist: Michelle Biedscheid

Timeline photo credits: Library of Congress (top right);
Shutterstock/Johnny Lye (top left), skvoor (middle left);
Sports Illustrated/John Biever (bottom right), John W.
McDonough (bottom left).

Library of Congress Cataloging-in-Publication Data is
available on the Library of Congress website.

ISBN: 978-1-4342-2227-5 (library binding)
ISBN: 978-1-4342-3076-8 (paperback)

Summary: Danny learns to use his speed as an asset
in wrestling.

Printed in the United States of America in Stevens Point, Wisconsin.
072011   006298R

TABLE OF CONTENTS

Danny Gohl

Wrestling

AGE: 10
GRADE: 4
SUPER SPORTS ABILITY: Super speed

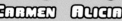 **CARMEN** **ALICIA** **JOSH** **DANNY** **KENZIE** **TYLER**

VICTORY SCHOOL MAP

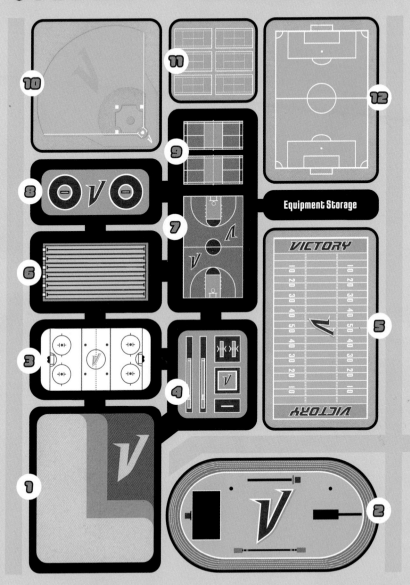

1. Main Offices/Classrooms
2. Track and Field
3. Hockey/Figure Skating
4. Gymnastics
5. Football
6. Swimming
7. Basketball
8. Wrestling
9. Volleyball
10. Baseball/Softball
11. Tennis
12. Soccer

Equipment Storage

Stuck in a Cradle

Sometimes having super speed is great. I can blaze through chores or zap video game aliens before they even see me coming. It's also great for football, especially when you're a running back like me.

But today, being fast isn't helpful — not when I'm stuck in a cradle.

Here's what happened. One of the wrestlers on the Victory School team had to drop out because his family was moving away. Coach Hayes, who coaches wrestling, asked me to join the team.

Now the big tournament is only a week away, and we don't have much time to prepare. We're drilling hard every day. There's no time for mistakes.

For practice, I'm wrestling Brock. He's one of the best wrestlers on our team. His arm tightens around my neck like a vise. I try to remember the wrestling DVDs Coach gave me to watch and the drills we did.

What were the moves? There was the
ankle pick, fireman's carry, monkey tail,
half-nelson, and of course, the cradle. Ugh!
I think I read everything too fast. It's all
jumbled up in my brain.

I feel Brock exhale and loosen his grip.
I slip free. Then I zip around him — fake
left, fake right — just like on the football
field.

"No, no, no!" Coach Hayes shouts. "Danny, it's a wrestling mat, not a dance floor."

It's never good when Coach calls you out. Now my *stomach* feels like it's in a cradle.

"Don't worry about it," Brock says. That's easy for him to say.

I head to the bleachers where my stuff is, and I slip on my sweats.

Just then I hear laughter. I look up and see my sister, Alicia, standing by the bleachers. The rest of her cheer team is there, too.

Alicia tosses her head back and laughs harder. My cheeks burn. My face feels like it's on fire. I hate being laughed at.

I march over to her. "So I'm terrible at wrestling," I say. "Go ahead and make fun of me. Go ahead and laugh!"

Alicia looks surprised and starts to say something, but it's too late. I'm gone. She could never catch me, even if she had a fifty-yard head start.

I dash out of the gym and across the nearby football field, my legs pumping like pistons. Running always makes me feel better.

I'm blocks away from school *and* Alicia, but I keep running. Usually a good run is all I need to clear my head. But today, I can't stop thinking about everything.

Coach and the other guys say they know I'll learn the moves and help the team win. I'm not so sure.

Being fast comes naturally to me. That's why I'm at the Victory School for Super Athletes. The kids at Victory all have extreme abilities, like my super speed. But what good is speed in wrestling?

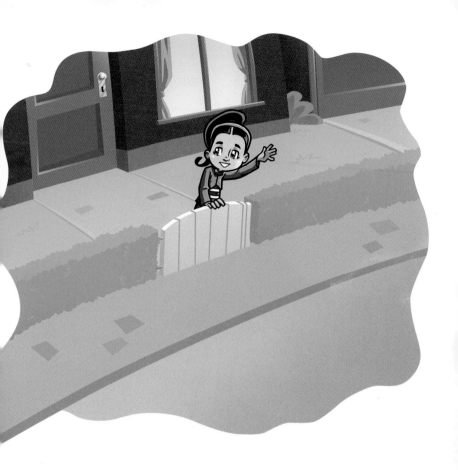

Suddenly, I hear a familiar voice. I've only been running a minute, but I'm already at my friend Kenzie's house. And she lives almost a mile from school!

Kenzie flags me down. "Hey, Danny, what's up?" she says.

"Not much," I say. I'm not even winded. I could run forever.

Kenzie walks up to me. She locks her arms around me in a bear hug. I feel like a soda can about to be crushed. She's squeezing me so hard.

"Hey, Danny," she says, "I hear you're on the wrestling team. But can you get out of my famous Kenzie Krusher hold?" She laughs.

I know she is joking, but I don't think she is very funny. "Ha, ha, Kenzie. Very funny," I say. "You know because of your super strength I can't break your hold."

I try to get my arms loose, but it's like I'm wrapped in a steel blanket.

"KENZIE!" I shout.

"Danny, don't get so mad," Kenzie says. "I was just kidding around."

She lets go, and I can breathe again. I rub my arm and shoot her a mean look.

"Sorry," she says, "I guess you're not in the mood for jokes."

That's the understatement of the year. I wave Kenzie off and start running again.

Whoosh! I'm home in less than two minutes.

CHAPTER 3

Feeling Jumpy

As soon as I hit the door, I smell something great. It's the sweet smell of cookies. Mom's baking a batch of double chocolate chip, my favorite. They're not done yet, so I race to my room to change clothes.

I feel extra jumpy, and I just can't sit still. I try doing homework. But I keep racing over the pages, reading the same sentence ten times. Math doesn't go any better.

I better wait on the studying. I just can't calm myself down, and I've learned before that it never pays to rush through your homework.

I get up and stretch. Then I play a video game. Then I watch some TV. I'm bouncing around the house like a pinball.

Alicia walks in the room. She starts to say something. But I'm so jumpy that I can't stop to listen. Instead, I breeze past her and head for the kitchen.

I grab a plate and pile it with cookies.
I plop down to enjoy the warm gooey
goodness. Wrestling moves run through my
mind.

Moves from the bottom position: escape and
reversal. Moves from the top position: chicken
wing and monkey tale. Basic takedown moves:
ankle pick, single-leg takedown, and double-leg
takedown.

I look at the empty plate. Oh, my gosh!
I've just downed eight cookies.

"Daniel Gohl!" says Mom. "Why did you
eat all those cookies so close to dinnertime?
You'll spoil your appetite."

Too late, I think to myself.

"Well, young man," Mom says, "what
do you have to say for yourself?"

"BURP!" Oops! That big burp just slipped out of me.

"I'm sorry," I say. "I didn't mean to."

Then I slip off to my room before Mom can give me a lecture. Thunderbolt, my dog, jumps up on the bed.

"Come here, boy," I say, scratching his neck. "I need a little wrestling practice."

I gently wrap my arm around his furry back. "Got you in a headlock," I say. "Ha! You're no match for my skills."

Thunderbolt slips free and pounces on my head, licking my face.

"Ugh! You got me!" I say, laughing. Thunderbolt can always cheer me up.

Skipping Practice

The next day at school, I'm running around the track. Unfortunately, I'm supposed to be at wrestling practice. I'm on my sixth lap when Alicia and Tyler, a basketball player, spot me.

"Coach is looking for you," Tyler says.

"You're in trouble, brother," Alicia adds. "Big time."

My eyes narrow. "Maybe you should laugh at me like you did yesterday," I say.

"What?" Alicia yells. "Stop running, and talk to me for a minute! When was I laughing at you?"

"At practice," I say. "You and the other cheerleaders."

"You mean in the gym?" Alicia asks. "Laurie told a joke, and we were all laughing at her, not you."

"Really?" I ask. I feel kind of dumb.

"Is that why you're here and not wrestling?" Alicia asks, her arms folded.

Now I feel *really* dumb.

"You better get to practice before Coach Hayes makes you do extra push-ups," Tyler says.

110 Percent

I sprint to the gym, where I see Coach sitting on a bench. He's watching the team do takedown drills.

"Nice of you to join us, Danny," Coach says. I can tell he's not happy. "You wouldn't think the fastest kid in school would be late," he adds.

"Sorry, Coach," I say. "Listen, maybe you made a mistake. Maybe you should pick someone else for the wrestling team."

Coach sits me down. "Danny," he says, "every kid at Victory is here because he or she can do something special. But it's not just about abilities. It's about character, too. About what's inside. They don't call it Victory School because you're a bunch of quitters."

I shuffle my feet nervously.

Coach continues. "I know you'll be a good wrestler. You're a team player and you always give 110 percent," he says.

"But how can super speed help me in wrestling?" I ask. "It's great for a running back, but a wrestler?"

Coach smiles. "You can't take down what you can't catch," he says.

A light bulb goes off in my head — just like you see in cartoons. Suddenly I know how to use my speed to win.

"I've got it!" I shout. "We start in the neutral position, both of us standing. Here's where my speed pays off. Before my opponent has a chance to react, I shoot in with a single-leg takedown."

I continue. "Then I spring on him, get him in a half-nelson, and go for the pin. Like you always say, Coach, 'Pin to win!' I'll be like a coiled snake, the poor guy won't know what hit him."

Coach pauses a minute. "Very good, Danny," he says, giving me a thumbs-up. "You probably won't get a pin that easily. But I like that you are thinking about how your speed can help you out there. You're going to do just fine."

CHAPTER 6

Takedown Artist

The next week flies by. I do drills with the other guys and work on my moves. The day of the tournament, I'm a little nervous. It's just like before a football game.

Coach stops by the locker room to give us one last pep talk. Then we walk out into the gym. It's more crowded than I expected. I scan the stands and see Kenzie and Tyler and my mom and dad.

Mom and Dad wave. Mom holds up
a sign that reads, "Danny: the Takedown
Artist." Man, I'm so embarrassed. But I
smile and wave back. It's nice to have them
rooting for me.

Alicia is with her squad. They're running
through their opening routine. Alicia does
a huge jump. I catch her eye, and she
winks at me.

In the first match my teammate Brock faces a really big kid. Brock's good, but I'm wondering if he can take down this giant.

The referee blows the whistle. Brock and Big Kid circle each other, looking for an opening. They clinch arms. Brock goes for the headlock hip-toss, a smart move. He grabs Big Kid by the arm and head and rotates his hip into his stomach.

Then Brock pops Big Kid over his hip onto the mat and lands on top of him. I guess skill counts for more than size in wrestling.

Before the end of the period, the ref is sweeping his hand, one, two, three times. *Bam!* The ref slams his hand on the mat, and we have our first win!

The crowd is on its feet, cheering. Coach grabs Brock and lifts him in a big bear hug. Our team is off to a great start.

Finally, it's my turn.

I hear my sister and her squad cheer: "Take 'em down, break 'em down, turn 'em over, pin! Let's go, Danny — we need a win!" Alicia can be pretty great sometimes.

I'm facing off against my first real opponent. He looks me over and sizes me up. "New kid, huh?" he says with a smirk.

Like a coiled snake, I say to myself.

I start in the neutral position then shoot in with a single-leg takedown, just like I've practiced. Yes! It works.

He's down — but not out. I'm working hard to get him in a half-nelson.

Coach was right. Pinning this guy isn't going to be as easy as I thought. But nothing worth doing ever is.

GLOSSARY

abilities (uh-BIL-i-teez)—skills or powers

appetite (AP-uh-tite)—hunger or a desire for food

character (KA-rik-tur)—the quality of having good morals and judgement

cradle (KRAY-duhl)—a wrestling hold in which one elbow is wrapped around the opponent's neck, the other elbow is behind the knee, and hands are clasped together so the opponent cannot move.

headlock (HED-lok)—a wrestling hold in which a wrestler locks his opponent's head between the crook of his elbow and the side of his body

opponent (uh-POH-nuhnt)—someone who is against you in a fight or contest

takedown (TAYK-doun)—a wrestling move in which one wrestler takes his opponent from a standing position down to the mat

tournament (TUR-nuh-ment)—a series of matches in which a number of wrestlers try to win first place

understatement (UHN-dur-state-muhnt)—a statement that is weaker or milder than what is actually true or happening

WRESTLING IN HISTORY

1896   The first modern **Olympic Games** are held in Athens, Greece. Wrestling is among the nine sports of the games.

1908   Iowan **Frank Gotch** beats Russian-trained **George Hackenschmidt** for the world heavyweight pro championship. Wrestling's popularity in the United States booms.

1921   The first high school state wrestling tournament is held in **Ames, Iowa.**

1972   Dan Gable wins Olympic gold. He does not give up even one point during the Games.

1984   The United States wins its first wrestling medals in modern Greco-Roman Olympic competitions.

1987   John Smith of Oklahoma State wins the first of six straight world freestyle titles.

1993   The United States wins its first-ever World Team Title in Toronto, Canada.

2004   **Women's freestyle wrestling** is added to the Summer Olympics.

2008   **Henry Cejudo** becomes the youngest American ever to win Olympic gold in wrestling at age 21.

Ames

VICTORY SCHOOL SUPERSTARS

Five Fouls and You're Out!

It's a Wrestling Mat, Not a Dance Floor

There's a Hurricane in the Pool!

There's No Crying in Baseball

Who Wants to Play Just for Kicks?

You Can't Spike Your Serves

Read them ALL!

STONE ARCH BOOKS
a capstone imprint